THOMAS' SNOWSUIT

A Note from Robert Munsch

A long, long, LONG time ago when I was in first grade, my class had 60 kids in it!

The teacher didn't read any books and neither did the kids. It was not fun.

Well, here is a book that is fun to read for both you and your grown-ups.

READERS RULE!

Before Reading

High-Frequency Words

Practice reading these high-frequency words in the story:

but her someone your

Meet the Characters

Get to know the characters from the story by looking at the pictures and names below:

Thomas

Thomas's mother

Teacher

Principal

Plural Words

When you want a word to mean more than one, you add an *s* to the end of the word. In this story, Thomas talks about his *friends*, which means he has more than one friend. Take a look at the words below and add an *s* at the end to mean more than one.

gift

plant

rock

chair

Out of all of these words, which one would you want more than one of? Why?

Phonics

There is an **S** sound at the beginning of the word **snowsuit**.

Can you make an **S** sound?

Pay close attention to the shape of your mouth as you make the sound. It might be helpful to make this sound while you look in a mirror to see the shape your mouth makes.

Try these different activities to help practice the letter **S** sound.

1. Take a close look around you and try to find three objects that start with the same sound.

2. Think of three other words that also start with the same sound. As an extra challenge, can you think of any words that end with an **S** sound?

3. A simple word that has the **S** sound at the beginning is the word **sir**. As you read this word, pay attention to the two other letter sounds in the word.

4. When two words rhyme, they have the same sounds at the end of the word. Take a look at the pictures below and point to any of the words that rhyme with **sir**.

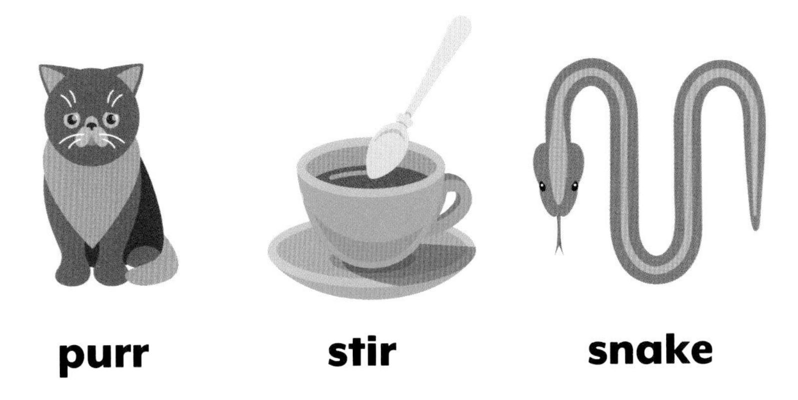

purr **stir** **snake**

5. While you read, look out for other **S** sounds at the beginning of a word throughout the story. You can see the sound easily because it will be written in a different color.

THOMAS' SNOWSUIT

Story by Robert Munsch
Art by Michael Martchenko

To Otis and Erika Wein in Halifax, who helped me make up this story, and to Danny Munsch

Thomas' mother said,

"Thomas, please put on your snowsuit."

Thomas said, "NNNNNO."

Thomas and his mother had a big fight.

When they were done, Thomas was wearing his snowsuit.

At school, the teacher said, “Thomas, please put on your snowsuit.”

Thomas said, “NNNNNO.”

Thomas and the teacher had
a big fight.

When they were done, the
teacher was wearing Thomas'
snowsuit and Thomas was
wearing the teacher's dress.

The principal came in and the

teacher said, “It’s Thomas!

He won’t put on his snowsuit.”

They all had another big fight.

When they were done,

Thomas and the teacher were

in their underwear.

So the principal said, “Thomas, put on your snowsuit.”

Thomas said, “NNNNNO.”

The principal picked up Thomas in one hand and he picked up the teacher in the other hand, and he tried to get them back into their clothes.

But when he was done, the teacher was wearing the principal's suit, the principal was wearing the teacher's dress, and Thomas was in his underwear.

Then the principal and the

teacher had a fight.

The principal wanted his suit.

The teacher wanted her dress.

Thomas watched the principal and the teacher have another big fight.

When they were done, everyone was wearing their own clothes.

From outside, someone said,

"Thomas, come and play."

Thomas ran to be with his friends.

Retell Activity

Look closely at each picture and describe what is happening in your own words giving as much detail as possible.

Clothing Designer

It's possible that Thomas didn't want to wear his snowsuit because he didn't like how it looked. Your challenge is to design a snowsuit that would be perfect for you!

- Think about some of the things that you love (e.g., rainbows, baseballs, trucks, cats), and make sure to include those ideas in the design of your snowsuit.
- Would you make your design a one-piece snowsuit, or two pieces with snow pants and a jacket? Why would you make that design choice?
- What other cool features would you add to your snowsuit to make it perfect for you? (e.g., extra padding on the knees because you love to build snow forts, an extra layer of warmth because you often feel cold, extra pockets for collecting things in nature)

Spot the Differences

Look carefully at the two pictures below.
Point to all the differences you can find.

1. The book color 2. Mom's skirt color 3. The shoe
4. Extra flowers 5. The missing flowerpot

Getting Ready for Reading Tips

- Pick a time during the day when you are most excited to read. This could be when you wake up, after a meal, or right before bedtime.

- Create a special space in your home for reading with some blankets and pillows. The inside of a closet, under a table, or under a bed can make the perfect cozy spot.

- Before you start reading, do a quick look at all the pictures and suggest what the story might be about.

- Can you find the part of the story that repeats?

- Can you add actions like claps, stomps, or jumps to match what is being said to make the words come alive?

- Try to use silly voices for the different characters in the story. Think about changing the volume (e.g., loud, soft), the speed you use to say the words (e.g., fast, super slowly), and how you say the words (e.g., like an animal, like a superhero, like someone older or younger).

- What makes this story silly or funny?

- What part(s) of the story would never happen in real life?

Collect them all!

Adapted from the originals for beginner readers and packed with **Classic Munsch** fun!

All **Munsch Early Readers** are level 3, perfect for emergent readers ready for reading by themselves—because

READERS RULE!

Robert Munsch, author of such classics as *The Paper Bag Princess* and *Mortimer*, is one of North America's bestselling authors of children's books. His books have sold over 80 million copies worldwide. Born in Pennsylvania, he now lives in Ontario.

Michael Martchenko is the award-winning illustrator of the Classic Munsch series and many other beloved children's books. He was born north of Paris, France, and moved to Canada when he was seven.

Designed by Leor Boshi

Thank you to Abby Smart, B.Ed., B.A. (Honors), for her work on the educational exercises and for her expert review.

Annick Press Ltd.

We acknowledge the support of the Canada Council for the Arts and the Ontario Arts Council, and the participation of the Government of Canada/la participation du gouvernement du Canada for our publishing activities.

Library and Archives Canada Cataloguing in Publication

Title: Thomas' snowsuit / story by Robert Munsch ; art by Michael Martchenko.
Names: Munsch, Robert N., 1945- author. | Martchenko, Michael, illustrator.
Description: Series statement: Munsch early readers | Reading level 3: reading with help.
Identifiers: Canadiana (print) 20220170991 | Canadiana (ebook) 20220171009 | ISBN 9781773216577 (hardcover) | ISBN 9781773216478 (softcover) | ISBN 9781773216713 (HTML) | ISBN 9781773216836 (PDF)
Subjects: LCSH: Readers (Primary) | LCGFT: Readers (Publications)
Classification: LCC PE1119.2 .M868 2022 | DDC j428.6/2—dc23

Published in the U.S.A. by Annick Press (U.S.) Ltd.
Distributed in Canada by University of Toronto Press.
Distributed in the U.S.A. by Publishers Group West.

Printed in China

annickpress.com
robertmunsch.com

Also available as an e-book. Please visit annickpress.com/ebooks for more details.